Dear Parents:

Congratulations! Your child is taking the first steps on an exciting journey. The destination? Independent reading!

STEP INTO READING® will help your child get there. The program offers five steps to reading success. Each step includes fun stories and colorful art or photographs. In addition to original fiction and books with favorite characters, there are Step into Reading Non-Fiction Readers, Phonics Readers and Boxed Sets, Sticker Readers, and Comic Readers—a complete literacy program with something to interest every child.

Learning to Read, Step by Step!

Ready to Read   Preschool–Kindergarten
• big type and easy words • rhyme and rhythm • picture clues
For children who know the alphabet and are eager to begin reading.

Reading with Help   Preschool–Grade 1
• basic vocabulary • short sentences • simple stories
For children who recognize familiar words and sound out new words with help.

Reading on Your Own   Grades 1–3
• engaging characters • easy-to-follow plots • popular topics
For children who are ready to read on their own.

Reading Paragraphs   Grades 2–3
• challenging vocabulary • short paragraphs • exciting stories
For newly independent readers who read simple sentences with confidence.

Ready for Chapters   Grades 2–4
• chapters • longer paragraphs • full-color art
For children who want to take the plunge into chapter books but still like colorful pictures.

STEP INTO READING® is designed to give every child a successful reading experience. The grade levels are only guides; children will progress through the steps at their own speed, developing confidence in their reading. The F&P Text Level on the back cover serves as another tool to help you choose the right book for your child.

Remember, a lifetime love of reading starts with a single step!

Visit us on the Web!
StepIntoReading.com
rhcbooks.com

Educators and librarians, for a variety of teaching tools, visit us at RHTeachersLibrarians.com

Library of Congress Cataloging-in-Publication Data
Names: Rosenthal, Amy Krouse, author. | Barrager, Brigette, illustrator.
Title: Uni the unicorn goes to school : an Amy Krouse Rosenthal book / pictures based
on art by Brigette Barrager.
Description: New York : Random House Children's Books, [2020] |
Series: Uni the unicorn | Audience: Ages 4–6 | Audience: Grades K–1 |
Summary: Uni is eager to learn how to use her horn to fix things, but her teacher,
Mr. Wise, says she must practice her magic and also use her heart.
Identifiers: LCCN 2019026343 (print) | LCCN 2019026344 (ebook) |
ISBN 978-1-9848-5027-0 (trade paperback) | ISBN 978-1-9848-5028-7 (library binding) |
ISBN 978-1-9848-5029-4 (ebook)
Subjects: CYAC: Magic—Fiction. | Helpfulness—Fiction. | Unicorns—Fiction. | Schools—Fiction.
Classification: LCC PZ7.R719445 Us 2020 (print) | LCC PZ7.R719445 (ebook) | DDC [E]—dc23

Printed in the United States of America
10 9 8 7 6 5 4 3 2 1

This book has been officially leveled by using the F&P Text Level Gradient™ Leveling System.

UNI
Goes
to
School

Uni the UVICORN

an Amy Krouse Rosenthal book
pictures based on art by Brigette Barrager

Random House 🏠 New York

It is Uni's
first day of school.
Uni will learn
unicorn magic.

Uni sits under
a special tree.

Unicorns can fix things
with their horns.

Uni wants to
learn how.

Oh, no!

A branch has fallen.

Uni wants to
fix the branch.

Then Silky, Goldie, and
Pinkie join Uni.
They hurry to school.

Mr. Wise
is their teacher.
"Today we will help out
in the forest,"
he says.

"I want to practice
unicorn magic,"
says Uni.
"I want to fix
my special tree."

12

"Magic is not easy," Mr. Wise tells Uni. "Let's look for animals who need our help."

Silky finds a turtle
on his back.
She flips him over
with her nose.

"Good job!"
their teacher says.
"Who is next?"

Uni shows them
the broken branch.
"I will put the branch
back on the tree
with magic."

Uni's horn taps
the tree trunk.
Nothing happens.

Next, a squirrel cannot
reach a nut.
Goldie knocks it down
with his horn.

"There goes
a happy squirrel,"
says Mr. Wise.
"Your turn, Uni."

"This time,
I will fix the branch,"
says Uni.

Uni's horn taps
the broken branch.
Nothing happens.

Then Pinkie sees a fox
stuck in a bush.
"Grab my tail," she says.
She pulls the fox free.

"That was kind,"
says Mr. Wise.
"Uni, will you
try again?"

Uni's head droops.
"I tried," Uni says.
"My horn
does not work."

"Magic takes practice,"
says Mr. Wise.
"But it also comes
from the heart."

Uni spots a nest.

There are eggs inside!

The birds are worried

about their eggs!

Uni will help them.

Uni gently taps

each egg.

Nothing happens.

Then . . .

there is a rainbow glow!

Sparks fly!

The broken branch
is as good as new.
The nest is safe.

The birds sing.

Uni's friends cheer.

Mr. Wise says,

"Way to keep at it, Uni!"

The eggs begin to crack.
The baby birds
are hatching!

Uni is so glad
to have helped
the birds.
Uni's heart glows!